ONE
IS A FEAST FOR MOUSE
A Thanksgiving Tale

by **Judy Cox**

illustrated by
Jeffrey Ebbeler

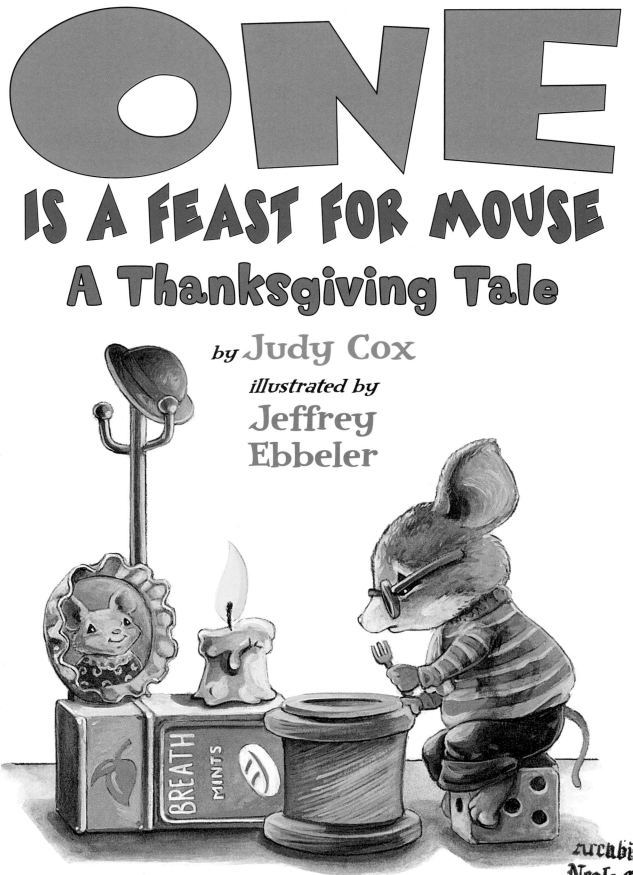

Holiday House / New York

To Mom and Dad
J. C.

For Kiera, Shannon, and James
J. E.

Library of Congress Cataloging-in-Publication Data
Cox, Judy.
One is a feast for Mouse: a Thanksgiving tale / by Judy Cox ;
illustrated by Jeffrey Ebbeler. – 1st ed.
p. cm.
Summary: On Thanksgiving Day while everyone
naps, Mouse spots one pea, a perfect feast,
but he cannot help adding all of the
fixings–until Cat spots him.
ISBN 978-0-8234-1977-7 (hardcover)
[1. Mice–Fiction. 2. Cats–Fiction.
3. Greed–Fiction. 4. Thanksgiving Day–Fiction.]
I. Ebbeler, Jeffrey, ill. II. Title.
PZ7.C838350n 2008
[E]–dc22
2007013972

After Thanksgiving
dinner Mouse crept out
of his hidey-hole and
looked around.

The house was quiet. Dad snoozed in his chair with his book. Mom dozed in front of the TV. Outside, the kids played football in the crisp yellow leaves. Cat curled up by the fire. He yawned and stretched his stripy tail. Then he closed his greeny eyes and went to sleep.

Mouse scampered up the tablecloth. Thanksgiving leftovers were still on the table. So much to eat!

Mouse saw a teensy-tiny, toothsome, green pea all by itself under a plate. Give thanks, he thought. One will be a feast for me.

Mouse rolled the pea across the tablecloth to take it back to his hidey-hole.

But his eyes were bigger
than his stomach. He saw six
leftover cranberries, glowing
like rubies on a silver saucer.
"I'll just take one," he said to
himself. "One is a feast for me."
He balanced one cranberry on
top of the pea and started once
again across the table to his
hidey-hole.

Just then he saw three olives, black and shiny, in a dish. I'll just take one, he thought. One is a feast for me.

He put the olive on top of the cranberry on top of the pea and carried the tidbits across the table.

Then he saw the carrot sticks, crunchy and munchy and orange.

I'll just take one, he thought. One is a feast for me. He stuck one carrot stick into the hole in the olive, balanced both on top of the cranberry on top of the pea, and started back to his hidey-hole.

Then he saw the mashed potatoes. Mouse potatoes! There was just one scoop left on the plate. I'll just take the plate, Mouse thought. What a feast I will have! He balanced the plate of potatoes on top of the carrot stick in the hole in the olive on top of the cranberry on top of the pea. Mouse started off across the table.

Then he saw the gravy,
brown and luscious, in the silver
gravy boat. Gravy for the mouse potatoes,
he thought. I must have that for my feast!
And he balanced the gravy boat on top of
the mashed potatoes on top of the carrot
stick stuck in the olive on top of the
cranberry on top of the pea. And he
started off. . . .

But then he spotted the pumpkin pie!
One slice of pie, brown and dimpled, with a collar
of fluffy cream.

So he balanced the pie
on top of the gravy boat
on top of the mashed
potatoes on top of the
carrot stick stuck in
the hole in the olive...

on top of the
cranberry on
top of the pea,
and he started off
across the table.

The pie slid, but Mouse caught it just in time. Mouse bobbed and bobbled across the tablecloth on the way to his hidey-hole for his Thanksgiving feast. He didn't see Cat creeping, creeping closer and closer.

But Mouse
saw the turkey!
Brown and juicy,
surrounded
with parsley. Much
was gone, but there
was enough left for
a mouse feast—or even
two! I'll just add that,
thought Mouse. And he
carefully placed the turkey
platter on the very top of his
pile. On top of the pie on top
of the gravy on top of the
mashed potatoes on top of
the carrot stick stuck in the
hole in the olive on top of the
cranberry on top of the pea.

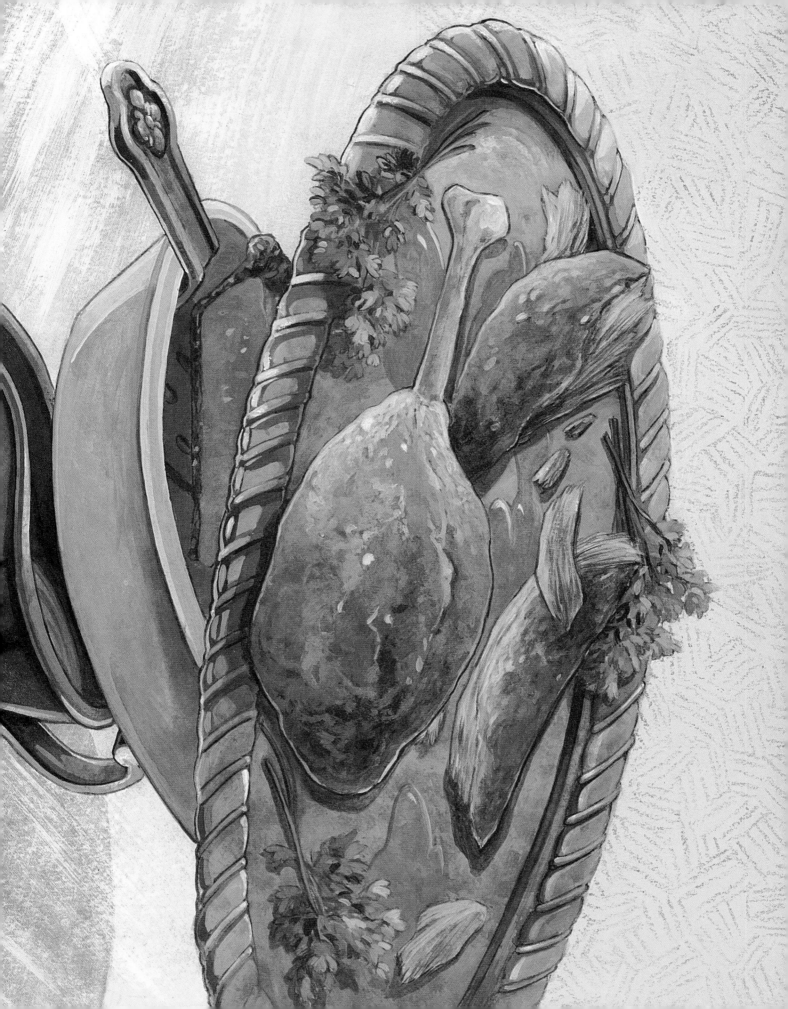

He started off across the table to his hidey-hole.
And there, at the table's edge, he met **Cat**,
greedy eyed and hungry, clawing up the table
on the tablecloth.

Mouse skidded to a stop. The turkey wibbled and wobbled, slid and slipped. Mouse danced to keep his feast balanced, pirouetted like a ballerina, juggled like a platter-spinner!

But off slid the turkey! WHOOSH! With a PLOP! Landing smack on Cat.

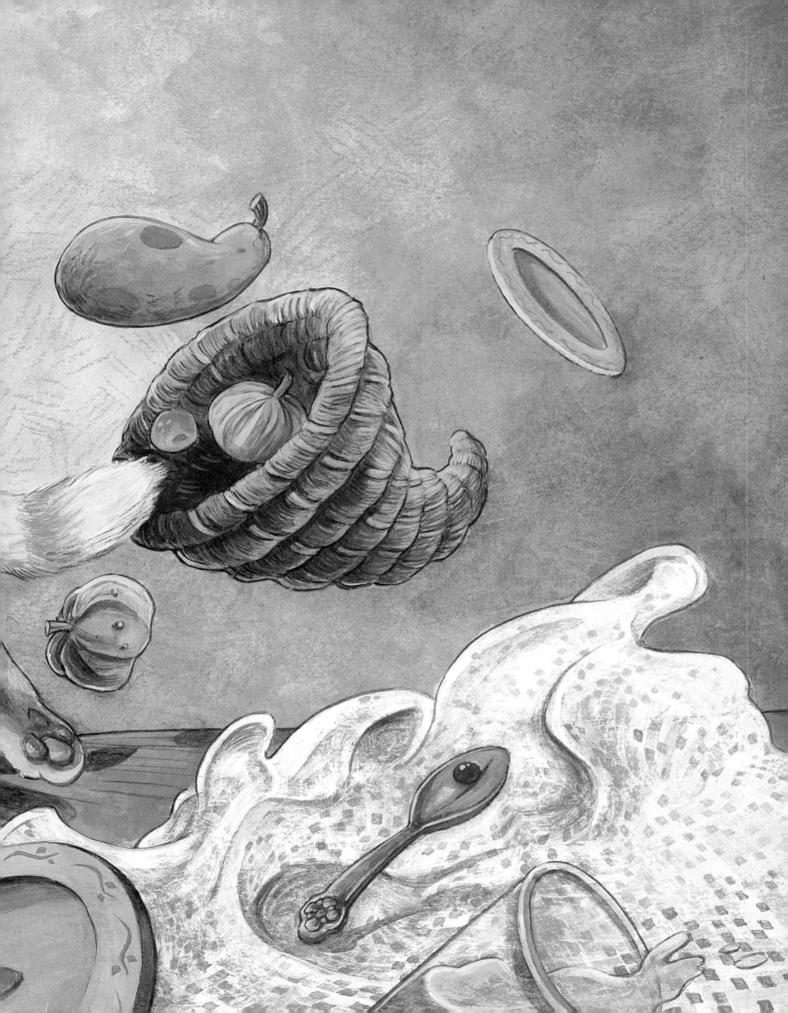

Down crashed the
pumpkin pie and the boat
with the gravy. Down crashed
the mashed potatoes with a clatter
that woke Mom! Down fell the carrot
stick, still impaled in the olive! Down went the
cranberry, which rolled, leaving a red track
across the tablecloth! Down went the pea, all
catter-whumpus off the table, rolling onto the floor.
Off scampered Mouse, quick as
a bandit, back to his hidey-hole
ahead of Cat!

He huddled in his hidey-
hole. His heart pitter-
pattered. He peered out.
   Down came the broom on
the stripy, greeny-eyed cat.
   "Bad kitty!" shouted Mom.
"Outside!" And she swept
the cat out the door.
   Mouse looked around,
whiskers trembling with
fright. No Thanksgiving
feast for me, he thought.
Just then he spotted,
glowing in the corner . . .

. . . one teensy-tiny, round and toothsome, green and luscious pea.

"Give thanks! One is a feast for me!"